I've Lost My
HIPPOPOTAMUS

JACK PRELUTSKY

I've Lost My HIPPOPOTAMUS

MORE THAN 100 POEMS ILLUSTRATED BY
JACKIE URBANOVIC

Greenwillow Books
An Imprint of HarperCollinsPublishers

For Pam and Jack,
with love and laughter—J. U.

I've Lost My Hippopotamus. Text copyright © 2012 by Jack Prelutsky.
Illustrations copyright © 2012 by Jackie Urbanovic.
All rights reserved. Printed in the United States of America.
For information address HarperCollins Children's Books,
a division of HarperCollins Publishers, 10 East 53rd Street,
New York, NY 10022. www.harpercollinschildrens.com
Ink was used to prepare the black-and-white art.
The text type is Goudy Catalogue MT.

Library of Congress Cataloging-in-Publication Data

Prelutsky, Jack. I've lost my hippopotamus: poems / by Jack Prelutsky ;
illustrations by Jackie Urbanovic.
p. cm.
"Greenwillow Books."
ISBN 978-0-06-201457-3 (trade bdg.) —
ISBN 978-0-06-201458-0 (lib. bdg.)
[1. Children's poetry, American. 2. Humorous poetry, American.
I. Urbanovic, Jackie, ill. II. Title.]
PS3566.R36F33 2012   811'.54—dc22   2011002636

12 13 14 15 16 CG/WOR 10 9 8 7 6 5 4 3 2 1   First Edition
Greenwillow Books

In memory of Janet Schulman—J. P.

6.

I've Lost My Hippopotamus

I've lost my hippopotamus,
The situation's weird.
One minute she was next to me,
Then *poof!* she disappeared.
It's hard to lose a hippo,
For a hippo's truly huge—
I'm sensing something fishy,
Some unsavory subterfuge.

I've searched and searched with no success,
I've yet to find a clue
To her status or location,
I'm unsure of what to do.
If you spot a hippopotamus
Where usually there's none,
Please let me know, the odds are good
You've found my missing one.

The Fish Are in the Treetops

The fish are in the treetops
To greet the morning sun.
The owls are underwater,
Where they're learning how to run.
The cows have taught the elephants
To fly around for fun . . .
I hope things get more interesting
Before this day is done.

8.

The Scritchy Scratchy Scrootches

The Scritchy Scratchy Scrootches
That live in Scratchy Patch
Begin their scritchy scratching
The second that they hatch.
They scritchy scratch the flowers,
They scritchy scratch the trees.
They scritchy scratch all creatures
From elephants to fleas.

They're thoroughly unpleasant
In ways you can't ignore.
Their constant scritchy scratching
Is easy to abhor.
They're furthermore elusive,
So you can never catch
The Scritchy Scratchy Scrootches
That live in Scratchy Patch.

My Chicken

My chicken seems to think an egg
Exists for her to hatch it.
My puppy seems to think a bug
Exists for him to catch it.

My kitten seems to think her fur
Exists for her to lick it.
My brother seems to think his nose
Exists for him to pick it.

I'm Riding on a Snail

I'm riding on a snail
That's bigger than a horse.
We don't go very fast . . .
It's still a snail, of course.
We take about a month
To go about a mile.
When I'm riding on a snail,
Things tend to take a while.

Its only speed is slow,
But things could still be worse.
Imagine if the snail
Should go into reverse.
I try to speed it up—
It's all to no avail.
A trip takes extra time
When you are on a snail.

.13

I Love to Pet My Rabbit

I love to pet my rabbit,
She has exquisite fur.
I pet my pretty kittens,
They purr and purr and purr.
I pet my pudgy puppy,
Who wiggles with delight,
Then pet my little pony,
Which helps him sleep all night.

I pet my two canaries,
And soon they start to sing.
I even pet my turtle,
Who doesn't feel a thing.
I pet my hippopotamus,
Iguana, duck, and rat.
I never pet my porcupine—
I'm much too smart for that.

I'm Bouncing, Bouncing, Bouncing

I'm bouncing, bouncing, bouncing,
I'm bouncing in the air.
I bounce with little effort,
I bounce with little care.
My bouncing keeps improving,
I'm bouncing very high,
Attracting the attention
Of eagles soaring by.

I'm bouncing through the stratosphere,
I'm bouncing to the moon.
My mother may be worried
If I don't stop bouncing soon.
I'm bouncing, bouncing, bouncing
Exactly as I choose.
The secret of my bouncing
Is my brand-new bouncing shoes.

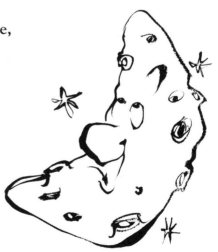

Otto Gottalott

My name is Otto Gottalott,
And I've got things that you do not.
I've got eleven lead balloons,
A sofa stuffed with figs and prunes.
I own a ten-ton tennis ball,
A frog that's forty-four feet tall,
A whistle that will make you sneeze,
A cottage made of cottage cheese.

I have a horn to wake the sun,
A horse to carry when I run,
A watch that keeps the time on Mars,
And marbles made of falling stars.
I own ten dancing centipedes,
Spaghetti that I grew from seeds,
An underwater easy chair,
And stacks of hippo underwear.

I've got, among my many things,
An octopus that sweetly sings,
A platypus that laughs and laughs,
A pair of tiny green giraffes.
Additionally, I possess
A million mice, no more, no less,
A block of ice that's always hot . . .
My name is Otto Gottalott.

An Antelope Was Feeling Ill

An antelope was feeling ill,
But to her great elation,
The doctor quickly healed her
With an anteloperation.

Burton

A rather large fellow named Burton
Decided to dress in a curtain.
As he walked down the road,
Quite a bit of him showed.
Of this we are practically certain.

Assorted Appleopards

Assorted APPLEOPARDS
Are dangling from a tree.
Though they appear delicious,
It's best to leave them be.
Do not approach too closely,
No matter how they purr,
And please do not be tempted
To stroke their rosy fur.

Do not attempt to pick them,
They are no simple snack.
If you should try to bite one,
It's sure to bite you back.
Enjoy them from a distance,
But if you hear them roar,
Turn tail and flee the forest—
They're beastly to the core.

ap-ill-EH-purdz

The Crabacus

Upon a beach, the CRABACUS
Is keeping careful count
Of every single grain of sand,
Recording the amount.

It's counted seven million
Seven hundred thousand ten,
But now the tide reshapes the shore—
It must begin again.

CRAB-uh-cuss

My Brain Is Unbelievable

My brain is unbelievable
In every last respect,
Which leads to the uncanny,
Ineluctable effect
Of making everything I think
Infallibly correct.

I think of this, I think of that
The moment I awaken,
And I am never, never wrong . . .
This fact cannot be shaken.
I thought I made an error once—
But I was just mistaken.

I Painted a Rhinoceros

I painted a rhinoceros
That didn't seem to mind,
Till it noticed I was painting
On its sizable behind.

If Pigeons Weighed as Much as Pigs

If pigeons weighed as much as pigs,
And dragonflies were dragons,
If caterpillars were as big
As Conestoga wagons,
If alley cats were lion-size
And roared enormous roars,
I probably would soon surmise
That I should stay indoors.

My Snake Can Do Arithmetic

My snake can do arithmetic,
My snake is far from dumb.
My snake can take two numbers
And come up with a sum.

She can't subtract, which makes her sad,
And two things make her sadder . . .
She can't divide or multiply—
My snake is just an adder.

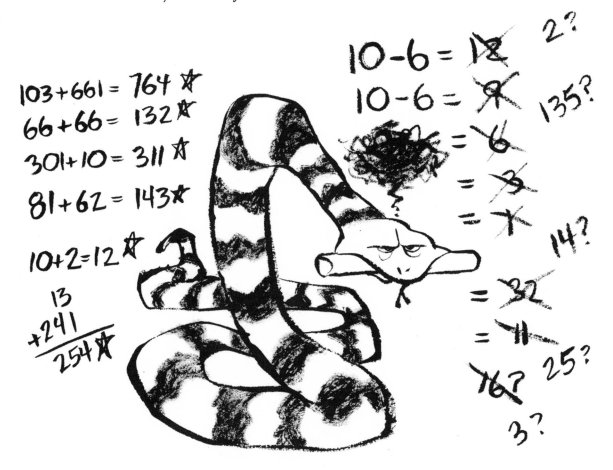

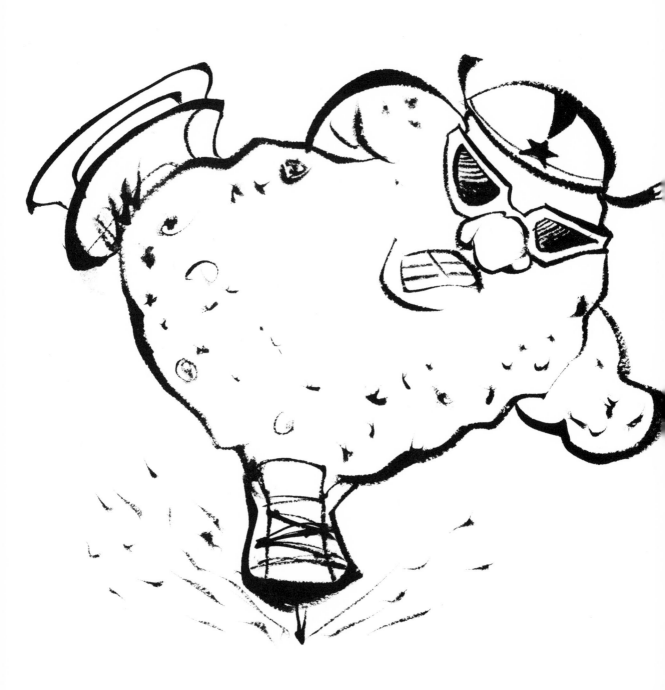

The Fabulous Skating Potato

I'm the Fabulous Skating Potato,
The swiftest potato on ice.
You'll not find a fleeter potato
At any location or price.
I circle the track with abandon,
Gathering speed as I go.
I make other skating potatoes
Appear to be woefully slow.

I've won many medals and trophies
For triumphing race after race,
Outdistancing lesser potatoes
Who couldn't compete with my pace.
My skating technique is perfection,
My moves are entirely precise.
I'm the Fabulous Skating Potato,
The swiftest potato on ice.

Shopping at a Dragon Store

I'm shopping at a dragon store
To see if I can find
The dragon I've been looking for,
A very special kind,
A dragon of a certain size
That's not too big or small,
A dragon that has friendly eyes
And likes to fetch a ball.

They've dragons here of every sort,
Of every dragon breed.
But so far they've all fallen short
Of being what I need.
I see one sitting on his bed,
I do not know his name,
But when I pet his scaly head
He breathes a gentle flame.

I offer him a dragon snack
And play with him awhile.
I hug him and he gives me back
A little dragon smile.
Every second that we play
I like him more and more.
I'll take that dragon home today . . .
I love this dragon store.

I Planted a Whistle

I planted a whistle
And grew a flute,
I planted a shoelace
And grew a boot,
I planted a button
And grew a blouse,
I planted a whisker
And grew a mouse.

I planted a tire
And grew a truck,
I planted a feather
And grew a duck,
I planted a ribbon
And grew a hat,
I planted a claw
And grew a cat.

I planted a collar
And grew a coat,
I planted an anchor
And grew a boat,
I planted a sheet
And grew a ghost—
My beautiful garden
Is better than most.

A Curious Quandary

I'm in a c∩rio∩s q∩andary
That is giving me the bl∩es.
The tro∩ble, as no do∩bt yo∩'ve g∩essed,
Is how I write my ∩'s.
It's a p∩zzling sit∩ation
That keeps ca∩sing me to frown,
For every ∩ I ever write
Is always ∩pside down.

It's f∩rthermore misshapen,
Like a small, inverted bowl.
It's j∩st a bit ∩nsettling,
B∩t it's o∩t of my control.
I've a second tricky iss∩e now
As s∩rely yo∩ s∩rmise . . .
Besides my ∩'s, I'm stymied
By the way I dot my i's.

Short Song of the Hungry Bookworm

I love books. Yes, I love books.
Oh books, it's hard to beat you.
I give you long and loving looks,
And then I slowly eat you.

I'm Running Away from Home Today

I'm running away from home today,
I'm running away from home.
My mom and dad both made me sore,
And so I'm heading out the door.
I will not live here anymore.
I'm running away from home today,
I'm running away from home.

I'm running away from home today,
I'm running away from home.
I washed my face, I combed my hair,
Then packed some socks and underwear,
And now without a single care
I'm running away from home today,
I'm running away from home.

I ran away from home today,
I ran away from home.
My little plan soon met defeat—
Besides not having much to eat,
I'm not allowed to cross the street,
So now I'm going home today,
So now I'm going home.

I Can Juggle Bowling Balls

I can juggle bowling balls
While standing on my head.
I can turn a butterfly
Into a loaf of bread.
I can catch a kangaroo
With nothing but a spoon
I can sing a song so loud
You'd hear it on the moon.

I can make a mountain range
Completely disappear,
While I ride a unicycle
And I rope a steer.
I can lift an elephant,
No matter what the size . . .
But most of all, what I can do
Is tell amazing lies.

The Gludus

The GLUDUS are a nuisance,
With a tendency to cling.
It's hard to make them go away,
They stick to everything.

If you should meet the GLUDUS,
There is little you can do.
You'll find that you are out of luck—
They'll soon be stuck on you.

GLUE-dooz

Wiguanas

WIGUANAS are dapper,
WIGUANAS are chic,
Each wearing a wig
That's completely unique.
They wander through woodland
Through valleys and glades,
In pigtails and ponytails,
Beehives and braids.

You'll find them on mountains,
On deserts and plains,
In Afros and Mohawks,
In colorful manes,
Conservative crew cuts
And intricate curls,
Elaborate hairdos
With billowing swirls.

In pageboys and topknots,
In rough, shaggy cuts,
Or styles that are apt
To remind you of mutts,
WIGUANAS possess
An unmatchable flair,
For they are the world's
Only lizards with hair.

wig-WAH-nuz

38.

The Halibutterflies

The HALIBUTTERFLIES
Are wondrous to behold,
They flutter through the skies
On wings of blue and gold.
We love their fishy heads,
Their iridescent scales,
And how, in flower beds,
They flash their fishy tails.

Of course, we understand
That half their time must be
Spent not above the land,
But underneath the sea.
We wait, and then we cheer,
For when that time is through,
They once again appear
On wings of gold and blue.

hal-ih-BUT-ur-flies

Most Ghosts

Most ghosts are insignificant,
Incalculably small.
It's impossible to find them,
Even when they caterwaul.

A number are voluminous,
A few are extra tall—
The enormous ELEPHANTOM
Is the grandest ghost of all.

R.I.P.

el-a-FAN-tom

I Peeled a Banana

I peeled a banana
And needed to sneeze.
I picked up a peach
And was bitten by fleas.
I gnawed on an apple,
My nose became numb.
My eyebrows fell out
When I swallowed a plum.

I ate a tomato
And started to weep.
I tasted an orange,
My feet fell asleep.
I looked at a lemon
And now I can't smile—
Perhaps I had best
Avoid fruit for a while.

Camel

I have one large hump,
Two long, beautiful lashes,
And a foul temper.

Frog

All evening I sing,
Happy on a lily pad,
Celebrating spring.

Mole

Tunnel! I tunnel!
I never see my tunnels,
Yet they comfort me.

Oyster

I'm clearly no gem,
But in my interior
I'm growing a pearl.

Peacock

I am glorious!
My tail has a thousand eyes
For you to admire.

Zebra

Black white black white black,
I am a striped illusion,
A horse in disguise.

We Hunt for Eggs on Halloween

We hunt for eggs on Halloween,
Unless it comes in May.
We give each other valentines
On Independence Day.

We sing some New Year's carols
On Thanksgiving, all week long.
My family loves the holidays
But gets a few things wrong.

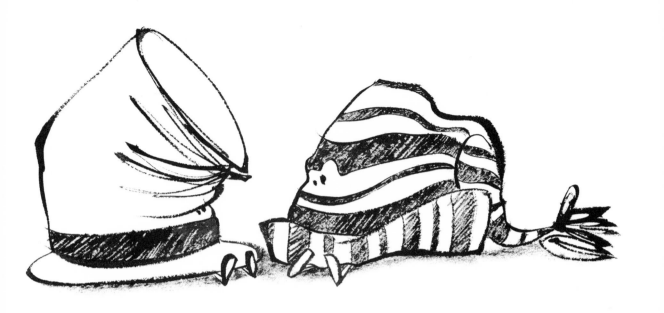

Two Hats Began a Journey

Two hats began a journey,
But they'd hardly gone a mile
When they started getting weary,
So they halted for a while.

Then side by side they rested
Till one hat arose and said,
"I'll let you nap a little more,
And I'll go on a head."

The Blumpazump's Birthday

Today's an auspicious occasion
That only occurs once a year,
A basis for great celebration,
And uncategorical cheer.
For today is the Blumpazump's birthday,
And as almost anyone knows,
The neighborhood gathers around her
To count her innumerable toes.

Of course, no one's ever been able
To tally the total amount,
For the Blumpazump never stops moving,
Thus thwarting an accurate count.
Yet none of them care in the slightest,
They don't think it matters at all.
They know what is really important
Is the Blumpazump's annual ball.

The neighbors are all in attendance,
It's truly a splendid affair.
The Brubbs rub their blubbery noses,
The Lubbs comb their lavender hair.
The Gliggs and the Sliggs sing in chorus,
The Grounts eat a mountain of cheese.
The Snoshes cavort in galoshes,
And the Twees uncontrollably sneeze.

The high point is right around midnight,
As festivities draw to a close . . .
The Blumpazump whirls with abandon
On the tips of her numerous toes.
The neighbors display their approval
With cheer after deafening cheer.
They wish that the Blumpazump's birthday
Took place more than one day a year.

The Fiff

If ever you should spot a Fiff
(Of which there are but few),
Then you're extremely fortunate . . .
Not many people do.
It's smaller than your fingernail
And doesn't make a sound,
So it's not easy to discern
When there's a Fiff around.

A Fiff is truly beautiful,
A gem of form and face.
It plainly is a pity
That it's not more commonplace.
But then again, because a Fiff
Is such a tiny size,
You'd be hard-pressed to notice it,
And you might strain your eyes.

One final fact about a Fiff
That you should know as well
Is that it manufactures
An insufferable smell.
If you detect an odor
That you'd rather never sniff
And cannot tell what's causing it,
It's probably a Fiff.

Tyrannosaurus and His Bride

Tyrannosaurus and his bride
Terrified the countryside.
Then they fell and broke their necks—
Poor Tyrannosaurus wrecks!

There Goes a Boomerangutan

There goes a BOOMERANGUTAN,
Encased in orange fur.
Curving swiftly through the air,
It's practically a blur.

A salient fact is known about
The BOOMERANGUTAN—
No matter when or where it goes,
It ends where it began.

boo-muh-RANG-uh-tan

.57

My Elephant Paints Pictures

My elephant paints pictures,
Gems of color, shape, and line,
Aesthetically superior
To every one of mine.
His drawings are exemplars
Of fluidity and grace.
I scribble worthless doodles
I should probably erase.

He shapes exquisite statues
Using nothing but his trunk.
I sculpt atrocious eyesores,
Unadulterated junk.
Though I lack his native talent,
Nonetheless I'm sort of smart,
So I've started taking lessons
From my elephant . . . in art.

58.

Two Sea Horses

Two sea horses sat on an undersea seesaw.
You see, they loved seesawing under the sea.
Those undersea sea horses seesawed and seesawed,
They seesawed with savor, they seesawed with glee.

Those seesawing sea horses seesawed all morning,
Then seesawed and seesawed from noon until four.
They seesawed so long they got seasick, so sadly
Those undersea sea horses seesaw no more.

Cupcakes

I'm very fond of cupcakes
And love to eat them up,
But I've never found a cupcake
That came inside a cup.

Lament of the Headless Horseman

I wish and wish and wish and wish
And wish I had a head.
I'm certain if I had one,
It would stand me in good stead.
I'd have a change of attitude,
For I'd feel more complete,
Plus people might not run away
When I ride down the street.

Because I do not have a head,
I also lack a nose,
And furthermore I'm mouthless—
Both conditions cause me woes.
It's odd that I can hear and see,
I've neither eyes nor ears.
I've never gotten used to this,
Although it's now been years.

I think that if I had a head,
The same as other folks,
I wouldn't be the target
Of intolerable jokes.
I'd finally have a need to put
A pillow on my bed,
And so I wish and wish and wish
And wish I had a head.

.63

On the Road to Undiscovered

ON THE ROAD TO UNDISCOVE

WORTHY DESTINATION. I SUSPECT I'VE GONE ASTRAY TO MY WAY TO THE FIND EVER I'LL IF WONDER TO BEGIN I EVEN EXISTS. IT THAT DOUBT MANY TRAVELED SELDOM VERY SO AND TWISTS, AND TURNS WITH

64.

WHERE SO FAR I'VE NEVER BEEN, I PEREGRINATE ENDLESSLY, MEANDER OUT AND IN. IT IS HARDLY EASY GOING, BUT I DO THE BEST I CAN. STILL, I SENSE I'VE MADE SCANT PROGRESS FROM THE SPOT WHERE I BEGAN. THE ROAD IS LONG AND ARDUOUS, REPLET...

Morton Short

My name is Morton Short,
I'm a noted worrywart,
I worry about things that might occur.
I worry that the stars
Will turn into candy bars,
So the skies will never be the way they were.

I worry that the seas
Will fill up with moldy cheese,
And furthermore I sit around and fret
As I ponder when my head
Will become a loaf of bread.
It's no wonder I am constantly upset.

I possess a deep concern
That one morning I will learn
Lovely butterflies now weigh a thousand pounds,
While chrysanthemums can roar,
Sweet narcissus snort and snore,
Thunder cannot even make the slightest sounds.

I've a never-ending fear
I'll inevitably hear
That giraffes have shrunk and now are very short,
That the planets, one by one,
Have stopped orbiting the sun . . .
I'm a worrywart, my name is Morton Short.

Observe the Strutting Stockingbirds

Observe the strutting STOCKINGBIRDS
Upon the avenue,
Displaying all their finery
For everyone to view.
No two of them are quite alike,
Each has distinctive legs,
Uniquely hued and patterned
Long before they leave their eggs.

They're proud and self-applauding
Of the way they are arrayed,
Explaining why they're often
On conspicuous parade.
They're pompous and ridiculous,
And far too vain for words,
But nonetheless we love to watch
The strutting STOCKINGBIRDS.

STOCK-ing-birdz

68.

Especially Serious Sam

I'm especially serious Sam—
Yes I am! Yes I am! Yes I am!
I have no desire to smile,
Not even once in a while.
My aspect's entirely severe,
I never know laughter or cheer.
Hilarity's not to my taste,
While whimsy is simply a waste.

I'm unsympathetic to fun,
And don't get the point of a pun.
Mere banter I cannot abide,
I haven't a frivolous side.
Don't bother displaying your wit,
I won't be impressed, not a bit.
Jocosity's truly a bore,
And horseplay I wholly abhor.

I'm somber, sedate, and intense,
So merriment doesn't make sense.
Caprice I dismiss and disdain,
It pains my so-serious brain.
You might as well jest with a wall,
A rug or a red rubber ball,
Tell jokes to an oyster or clam . . .
I'm especially serious Sam.

I Played a Game of Golf Today

I played a game of golf today—
I'd never played before.
I wasn't very good at it
And won't play anymore.

I shot a sixty-seven,
Which was surely not my goal.
My score was even higher
When I played the second hole.

The Pelicantaloupes

The PELICANTALOUPES,
Morose and melancholy,
Are predisposed to mope—
They're never very jolly.
Though graceful in the sky,
They're solemn on the wing
And almost seem to cry . . .
They've not been heard to sing.

They gorge from time to time
On marmalades and jellies.
This diet, while sublime,
Soon fills their melon bellies.
Their heads turn brilliant red,
Their melon bellies swell.
But still, this must be said—
They have a lovely smell.

peh-lih-CAN-tih-lopes

It's Raining in My Bedroom

It's raining in my bedroom,
So I'm getting soaking wet.
This is an odd phenomenon
I will not soon forget.
I have no upstairs neighbors,
So that cannot be the cause
Of this unexpected deluge
That descends without a pause.

It's raining in my bedroom,
Which I just don't understand,
For outside, not a single drop
Is watering the land.
Since I have no umbrella,
I've no way of staying dry
As those raindrops keep on falling
In unlimited supply.

I'm looking out the window,
There is not a sign of rain,
Yet it's pouring from my ceiling,
Which I simply can't explain.
I am getting inundated
By this never-ending tide.
There is only one solution—
I believe I'll go outside.

The Thopp

I spotted a Thopp
At the top of the dunes,
Trilling assorted
Unusual tunes.
Though I was unversed
In its musical choice,
I had to admit
That it had a fine voice.

The neighborhood birds
Were assembled around,
Enthralled by the sweet,
Unsurpassable sound.
Not one of them chattered
Or clattered its beak,
In awe of the Thopp's
Flawless vocal technique.

It sang a strange ballad
I'd not heard before.
It sang an old song
No one sings anymore.
It sang of the earth,
Of the sky and the sea,
As the birds listened closely
To each melody.

Then the Thopp slipped away
And it never returned,
But the birds put to use
The new skills they had learned.
And now through the day
Every one of them croons
A dulcet array
Of unusual tunes.

The Agile Hopalotamus

The agile HOPALOTAMUS
Possesses boundless grace.
It hop-hop-hops around the clock
From place to place to place.
It is dexterous, it is tireless,
And you quickly realize
It's unrivaled as a hopper
In defiance of its size.

The agile HOPALOTAMUS,
With consummate élan,
Hops higher and more often
Than all other hoppers can.
Everyone who ever sees it
Is indelibly impressed.
The agile HOPALOTAMUS
Is hopping at its best.

hop-a-LOT-a-muss

The Bridge to Nowhere

I crossed the bridge to Nowhere,
Which I'd heard of but not seen.
The second I arrived there
I was summoned by the Queen.
The Queen was doing nothing
At a rather rapid pace,
Which in Nowhere, I discovered,
Is the customary case.

She answered all my questions
Though I'd asked exactly none,
Yet I still knew next to nothing
When her answering was done.
I studied my surroundings . . .
There was not a lot to see.
Almost everywhere in Nowhere
Was invisible to me.

I noticed that the palace
Had no ceiling, floor, or wall
And that somehow I was standing
On not anything at all.
It was evident that Nowhere
Was like nowhere else I knew.
Though I wished that I were somewhere,
There was nothing I could do.

For the bridge I'd crossed had vanished
And was simply not around.
I searched everywhere in Nowhere,
It was nowhere to be found.
I am now marooned in Nowhere,
For no matter where I roam,
I can't find my way back somewhere . . .
Nowhere's feeling more like home.

Scary, Scary Monster Song

I'm a scary, scary monster
That loves to scare and scare.
I dress in scary sweater-vests
And scary underwear.
I'm scary every second
Of every single day,
And there is nothing you can do
To make me go away.

I have a scary posture,
I have a scary glare.
I often wear a scary hat
Atop my scary hair.
I'm scary, scary, scary,
I'm scary through and through.
I'm a scary, scary monster . . .
Boo! Boo! Boo!

My Weasels Have the Measles

My weasels have the measles
And my kudu has the flu.
My fleas and bees are sneezing
And my bluebird's feeling blue.
My kangaroo is jumpy
And my rabbit cannot hop.
My crickets have the hiccups,
Which they cannot seem to stop.

My beaver has a fever,
My chinchilla has a chill.
My quail and snail are ailing
And my eels are really ill.
My pony's growing hoarser
And my moose's tooth is loose.
My snakes have painful bellyaches,
Pneumonia plagues my goose.

My skunk has lost her senses
And my mole has caught a cold.
My elephant is wrinkling
Though he isn't very old.
My duck came down with chicken pox
And gave it to my gull—
It's grand to have so many pets,
My days are never dull.

I'm Gazing through My Telescope

I'm gazing through my telescope
At something in the skies,
Something I could never see
If I just used my eyes,
Something that's so far away
I wonder how the light
Can even reach my telescope
So I can see the sight.

Somewhere in the universe,
As distant as can be,
I know extraterrestrials
Are looking back at me.
Of course, I can't detect them,
And in fact, I have no hope.
If they can see me, they must have
A better telescope.

My Pig

My pig seemed somewhat crotchety
And generally miffed,
So I thought a new appearance
Might provide her with a lift.
I bought her fine cosmetics
And assorted beauty aids,
Which I applied strategically,
Along with beads and braids.

I powdered and perfumed her,
Which I hadn't done in years—
Festooned her tail with ribbons,
Fastened bangles to her ears.
I made her up with lipstick,
Rouge, mascara, and a wig.
The change is inexpressible . . .
She's now a perfect pig.

A Centipede Was Thirsty

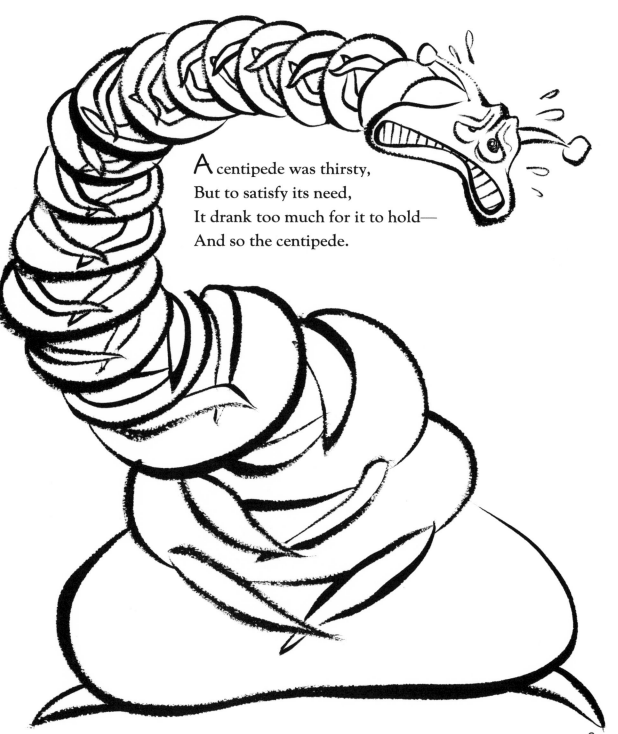

A centipede was thirsty,
But to satisfy its need,
It drank too much for it to hold—
And so the centipede.

I Cannot Sleep a Wink Tonight

I cannot sleep a wink tonight
And think that I know why—
My elephants are bellowing
In chorus to the sky.
My mice are misbehaving,
And my lions roar and roar.
My grizzly bears are wrestling,
Rolling all around the floor.

My kangaroos are boxing,
Knocking one another down,
My fatuous rhinoceros
Keeps acting like a clown.
My rats are racing all around,
My cats are giving chase,
Which causes a commotion
As they dart from place to place.

My monkeys yell, my donkeys bray,
My hawks and eagles shriek.
The din is indescribable
And possibly unique.
My pigs have started up a game
Of football with my sheep . . .
With such a loud menagerie,
It's hard to fall asleep.

Flamingoats

FLAMINGOATS are peculiar things,
They have two horns, they have two wings.
They sometimes fly, they sometimes trot,
They butt each other's heads a lot.

FLAMINGOATS squawk, FLAMINGOATS bleat.
FLAMINGOATS eat and eat and eat.
They congregate in noisy flocks
And scamper over stones and rocks.

They mill about on spindly legs,
Ignoring one another's eggs.
They preen their plumes and click their bills,
Then clamber up the steepest hills.

When they have reached the highest peaks,
They hurry down and eat for weeks.
They feast on straw and sticks and strings—
FLAMINGOATS are peculiar things.

fluh-MIN-goats

.87

A Wren Was Once a Tenant

A wren was once a tenant
In a little empty tent,
But then it was evicted
When it wouldn't pay the WRENT.

A Skinny Young Lady Named Grace

A skinny young lady named Grace
Painted a snail on her face.
She selected a snail
Though she'd wanted a whale,
But there simply was not enough space.

A Cowboy Had a Lazy Horse

A cowboy had a lazy horse
That didn't seem to know
That there was any other speed
But very, very slow.

One day that horse refused to budge,
It simply wouldn't go.
The cowboy couldn't coax it . . .
So ends this tale of WHOA!

The Afternoon My Hamster Died

The afternoon my hamster died,
I moped around and cried and cried,
Although I readily admit
That I was far from fond of it.
It was a poor, unpleasant pet
That I should probably forget.
It never had a proper name . . .
I miss it deeply, all the same.

My hamster had annoying ways—
A tendency to sleep for days,
A knack for making noise all night,
A need to gnaw, an urge to bite.
In fact, it bit me more than twice.
It simply wasn't very nice.
Despite these faults, I cried and cried
The afternoon my hamster died.

Let's Make as Much Noise as We Possibly Can

Let's make as much noise as we possibly can . . .
You bang on a pot and I'll clang on a pan.
We'll screech and we'll holler, we'll bellow and roar,
We'll jump up and down, and we'll stomp on the floor.

We'll thump on the ceiling, we'll bump into walls,
We'll shout out our lungs as we race through the halls.
It certainly sounds like an excellent plan
To make as much noise as we possibly can.

The Insufferable Asparagoose

The insufferable ASPARAGOOSE,
Unhappily, is on the loose.
A vagrant of some pantry shelf,
It makes a nuisance of itself.

A green, unappetizing fowl,
It wears an unremitting scowl
As all it does, day in, day out,
Is flap its wings and strut about.

Unpleasant, unappealing, mean,
It's but a blight upon the scene
That clearly is of little use—
I pity the ASPARAGOOSE.

a-SPAR-a-goose

I Got My Cat a Scratching Post

I got my cat a scratching post,
She simply didn't care.
She does her daily scratching
On the sofa and the chair.

I bought my dog a water bowl
Where he could drink his fill.
He still drinks from the toilet,
I suspect he always will.

I've asked them to behave themselves,
But both of them refuse—
And that's not even counting
What they both did in my shoes.

The Alligatorange and Crocodilemon

The ALLIGATORANGE
And CROCODILEMON
Are down in the swamp
On the lookout for food.
The fish in the swamp
Have a constant dilemma,
They're apt to be captured
And thoroughly chewed.

The ALLIGATORANGE
And CROCODILEMON
Are clever and patient
And watchful and sly.
They lurk in the shadows
To hide their bright colors,
Then happily swallow
Whatever they spy.

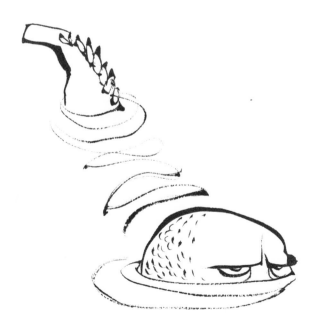

The ALLIGATORANGE
And CROCODILEMON
Are nasty and vicious
And sour and tart.
Stay clear of the swamp
That these creatures inhabit,
For though they look juicy,
They haven't a heart.

al-ih-gay-TAR-inge

crock-uh-die-LEH-min

I'm Knitting a Napkin of Noodles

I'm knitting a napkin of noodles,
Because I don't have any yarn.
I'm keeping my cow in the kitchen,
There's too little room in the barn.
I'm fishing with half an umbrella,
I don't have a suitable hook.
I'm reading the labels on light bulbs,
For somebody borrowed my book.

I'm building a boat out of bottles,
I've run out of lumber and nails.
I'm carrying sand in a trumpet,
I'm missing my buckets and pails.
I seem to be short of essentials . . .
In fact, I am lacking a lot.
But nevertheless I'm contented
And manage with what I have got.

A Baker Fell

A baker fell
Into a well
And nonchalantly said,
"I'll stay and wade
And ply my trade—
I'll bake the best well-bread."

My Octopus Is Different

My octopus is different
From most other octopi,
Not only can it sing and dance,
It's lately learned to fly.
I love to watch my octopus
Glide slowly overhead,
While crooning me a lullaby
Before I go to bed.

It cleans my room, so I don't have
To do it anymore.
It handles many brooms at once
And quickly sweeps the floor.
It helps me with my homework
And it even irons my shirts.
It shines my shoes, it combs my hair,
It serves me eight desserts.

My octopus is special
In innumerable ways.
It makes me tasty sandwiches,
Complete with mayonnaise.
It writes French, Czech, Italian, Thai,
Dutch, English, Hebrew, Greek . . .
It's nice to have an octopus
So thoroughly unique.

A Dozen Buffalocusts

A dozen BUFFALOCUSTS
Are swarming in the sky.
They chirp and snort in chorus
As they wing swiftly by.

When they are tired of flying,
They land in close array,
Then stamp their hooves with pleasure,
And graze throughout the day.

buh-fuh-LOW-kists

The Kangarulers

The KANGARULERS bound about,
And measure as they bound.
They cannot keep from measuring
Whatever is around.
They measure trees, they measure fleas,
They measure candy bars.
If they could jump up high enough,
They'd measure all the stars.

They measure every single thing
They ever come across.
They measure ham, they measure jam,
They measure applesauce.
There's nothing else the KANGARULERS
Seem to want to do.
So be prepared, there's little doubt
They're out to measure you.

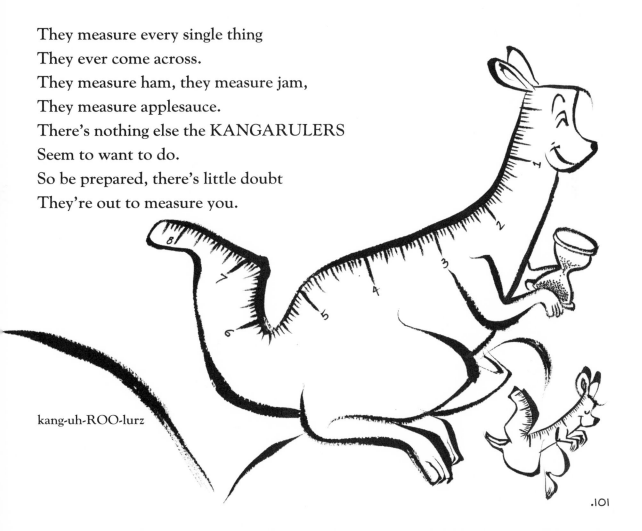

kang-uh-ROO-lurz

.101

The Penguinchworms

The PENGUINCHWORMS,
As white as rice,
As black as coal,
As gray as mice,
Hatch silently,
Then leave their eggs,
Undaunted by
Their lack of legs.

They cannot swim,
They cannot fly,
And sensing this,
They never try.
They inch along
An icy floe
And shiver softly
As they go.

In wind and snow,
On harsh terrain,
They wind their way
And don't complain.
They have no other
Stratagem . . .
And that is all
We know of them.

PEN-gwinch-worms

A Vegetable That Few Have Seen

A vegetable that few have seen,
Extremely leafy, brilliant green,
May be the only plant that grows
With an effective, working nose.

Whenever there's a sudden breeze,
It has a tendency to sneeze,
Which other plants can't hope to do—
That's why it's called the SPINACHOO.

SPIN-a-choo

GESUNDHEIT!

Pigeons

Pigeons are fine
When they're just looking at you.
Pigeons are pests
When they're perched on a statue.

Bongo Boo

O Bongo Boo, dear Bongo Boo,
I'm not a bit afraid of you.
I do not dread your razor teeth,
The ten above, the twelve beneath.
The menace of your rapier claws
Does not give me the slightest pause.
Though they might slice a stone in half,
The sight of them just makes me laugh.

As far as I can tell, your tail,
Though massive, is of no avail.
I giggle at your gruesome scowl,
Your wretched breath, your horrid howl.
In fact, I find your famous roar
Begins to bore me more and more.
So Bongo Boo, dear Bongo Boo,
I'm not a bit afraid of you.

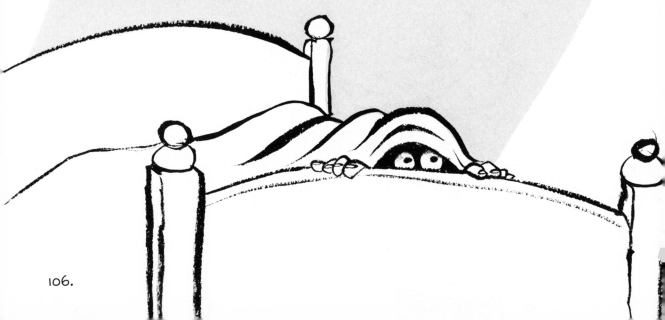

A Couple of Silkworms

A couple of silkworms decided
To race one another one day.
In spite of their mightiest efforts,
Neither one ever held sway.

The pair wiggled equally slowly,
Failing to show any speed,
So after a number of hours
Neither one managed to lead.

They finally gave up around sunset,
When most of the day had slipped by.
The outcome was unsatisfactory—
The duo wound up in a tie.

I Laugh at My Hyena

I laugh at my hyena,
My hyena laughs at me.
We entertain each other
And laugh incessantly.
It's clear that my hyena
Has a happy attitude,
For every time I've seen him
He's been in a foolish mood.

I laugh at my hyena
Until my sides are sore.
Then my hyena tickles me
And I laugh even more.
The two of us can't help ourselves,
We laugh and laugh and laugh.
I'm glad that I adopted him—
Instead of the giraffe.

The Screaming Weemies

We are the Screaming Weemies,
We scream and scream and scream.
We scream on all occasions,
We scream to let off steam.
It's hard to be around us,
Our screaming is intense.
Most people think our screaming
Makes very little sense.

We are the Screaming Weemies,
We have enormous throats
That amplify our screaming
And enable blaring notes.
We scream at everybody,
We scream at everything.
We probably keep screaming
Because we cannot sing.

My Pencil Will Not Write

My pencil will not write,
My crayons do not draw,
My lantern cannot light,
My saws refuse to saw.
My toothbrush is too soft,
My football can't hold air,
My kite won't stay aloft,
I've lost my underwear.

My songbird has no song,
My yo-yo doesn't work,
My calendar is wrong,
My clock has gone berserk.
My TV won't turn on,
My hat falls off my head,
My cat's meow is gone—
I'm better off in bed.

Mister Snoffle

Mister Snoffle made a waffle,
But the waffle turned out awful.
It was such an awful waffle
He refused to eat a bite.
Mister Snoffle, looking woeful,
Said, "This waffle is so awful
That it ought to be unlawful,
Now I'll make a waffle right."

Mister Snoffle was unruffled
As he made another waffle
Which was not the least bit awful . . .
For a waffle it was fine.
Mister Snoffle was more careful
In the crafting of this waffle,
And he laughed, "I'm feeling gleeful,
My new waffle is divine."

.111

Thanksgiving Math

I swallowed a third of the turkey,
A tenth of the carrots and peas,
A quarter of half the potatoes,
A fifth of a ninth of the cheese,
A sixth of an eighth of the pudding,
A seventh of all of the cake,
And so I am now doubled over
With triple a whole bellyache.

The Spotted Pittapotamus

The Spotted Pittapotamus
Lurks on a rocky shelf,
And if you do not spot it first
You're in a spot yourself,
For it has a pesky penchant
To precipitously pounce
On unprepared pedestrians
And eat them, ounce by ounce.

This procedure is unpleasant,
As it takes a month or two
Till you're thoroughly digested
And there's nothing left of you.
When passing through its territory,
Watch the rocks a lot,
For the Spotted Pittapotamus
Is difficult to spot.

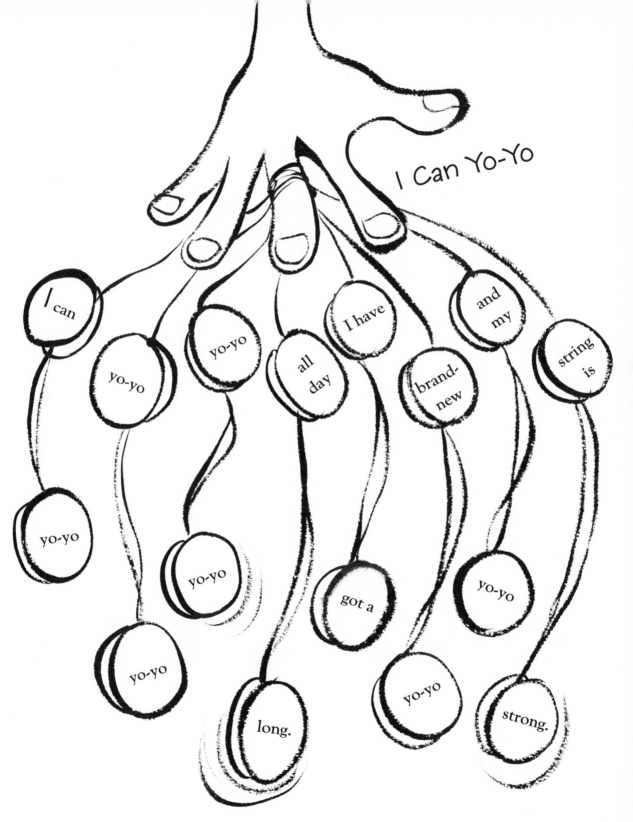

I Can Yo-Yo

I can
yo-yo
yo-yo
all day
I have
and my
brand-new
string is
yo-yo
yo-yo
got a
yo-yo
yo-yo
long.
yo-yo
strong.

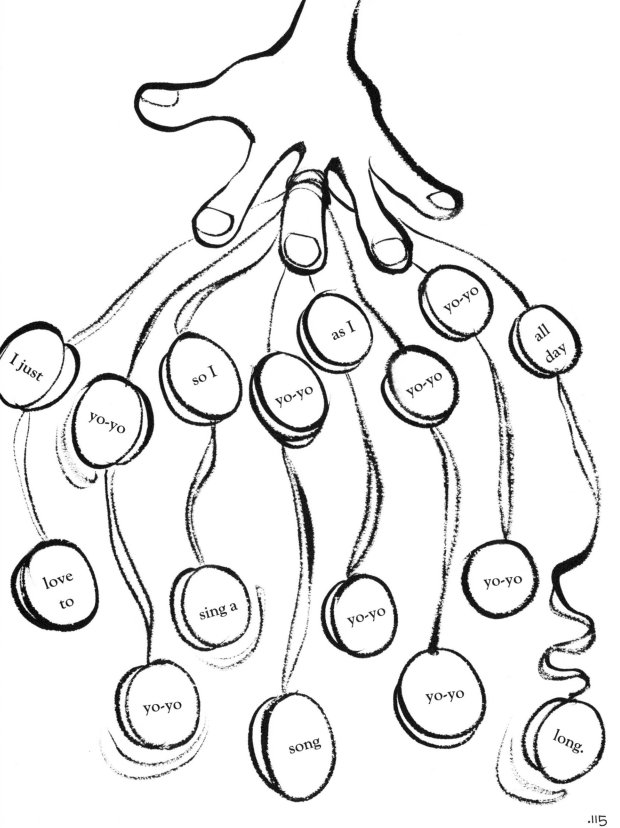

.115

The Troll's Not at the Bridge Today

The troll's not at the bridge today
To charge his normal fee.
The troll's not at the bridge today,
I get to cross for free.
The troll's not at the bridge today,
It's sort of a relief.
The troll's not at the bridge today . . .
He always gives me grief.

The troll's not at the bridge today,
He's simply gone away.
The troll's not at the bridge today,
I hope the troll's okay.
The troll's not at the bridge today,
I miss his growl and cough.
The troll's not at the bridge today—
Today's the troll's day off.

.117

Cormoranteaters

When CORMORANTEATERS are hunting for ants,
They spot them with merely a casual glance.
The ants try to hide, though it's well understood
That none of their efforts will do any good.

As CORMORANTEATERS descend through the skies,
Uncountable ants bid their final good-byes.
They know they have hardly a hint of a chance
When CORMORANTEATERS are hunting for ants.

CORE-mur-an-tee-turz

The Elegant Bowtiger

The elegant BOWTIGER
Is impeccable and svelte
In the sleek and stylish bow tie
That makes up its perfect pelt.
It pads about the jungle
With unmitigated grace,
A look of equanimity
Upon its noble face.

If you should note its bow tie
Is unknotted or askew,
There's one thing you should never,
Never, never, never do.
That is, of course, to tell it
There's a problem with its tie—
If you've observed its claws and jaws,
You probably know why.

bo-TIE-gur

A Gruesome Goblin

I am a gruesome goblin,
The meanest on the scene.
My gobliny complexion
Is uniformly green.
My nose is long and pointy,
My ears are pointy too.
My fangs are always ready
To take a bite of you.

I am a gruesome goblin
With mischief in my eyes.
I love to lurk in shadows
And catch you by surprise.
I have an awful odor,
An unattractive voice.
I'm nasty and annoying
By nature and by choice.

If I Don't Eat My Vegetables

If I don't eat my vegetables,
Like broccoli and peas,
My mother says I'll start to grow
Potatoes on my knees.
My toes will turn to cantaloupes,
My ears will fill with salt,
My nose will fill with pepper,
And it all will be my fault.

If I don't eat my vegetables,
My mother has no doubt
I'll lose my belly button,
And my teeth will soon fall out.
I also have to finish them
To prove I love her cooking.
And so I eat my vegetables—
But only when she's looking.

My Stomach, Every Now and Then

My stomach, every now and then,
Decides to sing aloud,
Which quickly draws a curious,
Enthusiastic crowd.
The music's unpredictable,
Each note is a surprise.
The songs are strangely out of tune
And hard to recognize.

My stomach's voice is squeaky,
Yet astonishingly strong.
No wonder people marvel
When it plunges into song.
Though I'm certain that a stomach
Is a necessary thing,
Nonetheless I'm disconcerted
When my stomach starts to sing.

It's Noisy in My Garden

It's noisy in my garden
And my ears are getting sore—
My tulips talk incessantly,
My dandelions roar.

.125

The Spellican

The SPELLICAN
Is a most talented bird
That's able to spell
Any difficult word.
It can spell *statuesque*,
It can spell *licensees*,
And even *synthetic*
With errorless ease.

But oddly, the SPELLICAN
Simply cannot
Spell three-letter words
Such as *dog*, *cat*, or *dot*.
In spite of this glitch,
Which is slightly absurd,
The SPELLICAN still
Is a capable bird.

SPELL-ih-kin

126.

The Ornery Pack Rattlesnake

The ornery PACK RATTLESNAKE
Takes all the trinkets it can take
And stores them in its shady lair,
Assured they are protected there.
It has a pair of bulging eyes
That help it find the smallest prize,
And when it spies a shiny stone,
It quickly claims it for its own.

The creature has a strange physique,
Its fur is long and soft and sleek.
Its sides are armored, scale on scale,
It has a rattle in its tail.
If it should give that tail a shake,
Don't bother the PACK RATTLESNAKE.
Just walk away without a fuss . . .
It is extremely venomous.

pack RAT-ill-snake

A Cricket in My Salad

I saw a cricket in my salad
And I heard the cricket chirp.
I was startled by the chirping
And it made me start to burp.

I'm so glad I found that cricket,
Now I keep it as a pet—
Plus its chirping and my burping
Make an excellent duet.

My Friend Pete

Though I'm impressed with my friend Pete,
Who plays the cello with his feet,
I'm dazzled by his sister Rose—
She plays the tuba with her nose.

The Busy Little Clipmunks

See the busy little CLIPMUNKS,
Clipping everything in sight.
They can clip a ream of paper
With one well-directed bite.
They love clipping things together—
Menus, memos, magazines—
We have seen them clipping bagels
To banana peels and beans.

They'll clip pencils to your pockets,
They'll clip feathers to your hair,
And if you should ask politely,
Clip them to your underwear.
If you have a thousand napkins,
They'll clip every single one. . . .
Call upon the little CLIPMUNKS
When there's clipping to be done.

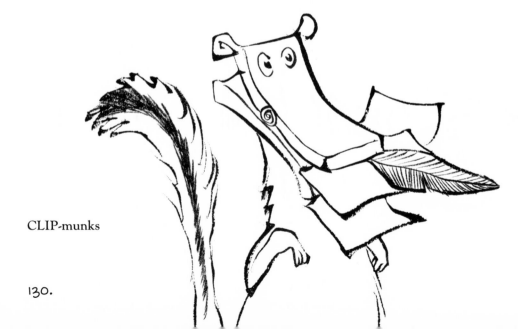

CLIP-munks

I Built a Robot Rabbit

I built a robot rabbit
That loved to race around.
It moved its feet so rapidly
They rarely touched the ground.

One day it self-destructed
From hopping far too fast.
I'll build a robot turtle . . .
Most likely it will last.

I Photographed an Onion

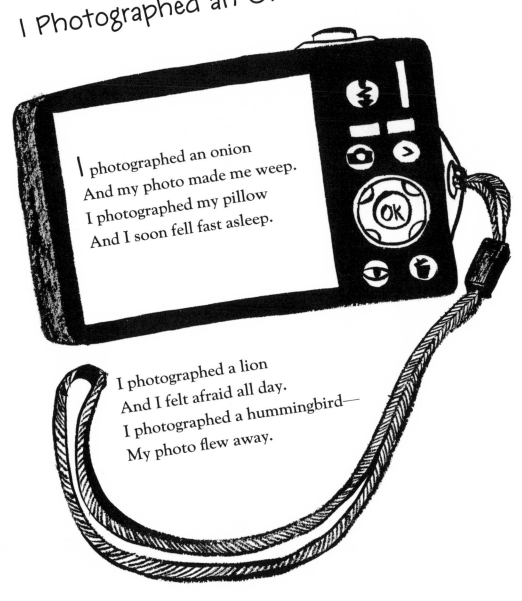

I photographed an onion
And my photo made me weep.
I photographed my pillow
And I soon fell fast asleep.

I photographed a lion
And I felt afraid all day.
I photographed a hummingbird—
My photo flew away.

The Alpacalculator

The ALPACALCULATOR is extremely erudite.
It calculates while grazing, and it grazes day and night.
It knows how many snowflakes are in fifty tons of snow
And what was in the ocean fifty million years ago.

There's nothing that the ALPACALCULATOR can't deduce.
It knows how many molecules are in a glass of juice.
It even knows how many stars exist in all creation—
It knows this all through complicated alpacalculation.

al-puh-cal-cue-LAY-tur

My Brother Has a Habit

My brother has a habit
He's been practicing for years.
He takes a pair of French fries
And sticks them in his ears.
He won't say why he does it,
And may not even know.
It's just a thing my brother's done
Since very long ago.

It's slightly gross, it's silly,
And obviously strange,
But once you have a habit
It's difficult to change.
He's lately added something
Even grosser, I suppose—
He also takes two French fries
And puts them in his nose.

When

When an orange needs assistance,
Do you give the orange aid?
When you argue with your footwear,
Do you think your shoes are swayed?
When you use no herbs in cooking,
Do you hope you're saving thyme?
When a lemon's green and tiny,
Does it seem a bit sublime?

When an apple joins the army,
Is it in the apple corps?
When a hog runs into traffic,
Could it be a crashing boar?
When you grab the wrong potato,
Do you take a different root?
When you're aiming at your laundry,
Are you on a laundry shoot?

When a carton casts a shadow,
Might it be a shadow box?
When you try selecting salmon,
Are you really picking lox?
When a beehive has no honey,
Then where can the honey be?
If you've never seen the ocean,
Do you have to go to see?

When you waltz on glowing embers,
Do you dance on daring feet?
When you need to eat a turnip,
Do you get to skip a beet?
When there's trouble at the circus,
Does it make the circus tense?
When your pocket's out of pennies,
Are you lacking common cents?

Index to Titles

Index to First Lines

Selected titles by Jack Prelutsky
published by Greenwillow Books